TEENAGE MUTANT NINJA TURLES™

Created by

Kevin Eastman & Peter Laird

TEENAGE MUTANT NINJA® TURTLES

GARY CARLSON
WRITER

FRANK FOSCO
PENCILLER

ANDREW PEPOY
ERIK LARSEN
CHANCE WOLF
INKERS

CHRIS ELIOPOULOS
LETTERER

ERIK LARSEN
EDITOR

REUBEN RUDE & I.H.O.C.
COVER COLORS

GARRETT CHIN
CHIEF EXECUTIVE

JOSH EICHORN
BONE SMUGGLER

TEENAGE MUTANT NINJA TURTLES® TRADE PAPERBACK. ISSUES 1-5. FIRST PRINTING. An Image Comics Group title published by Image Comics 1440 North Harbor Blvd. Suite #305 Fullerton, CA 92835. Printed in Canada.

ISBN 1-887279-56-3 $9.95 / $13.90 CANADA

image COMICS

LARRY MARDER
EXECUTIVE DIRECTOR

DOUG GRIFFITH
ART DIRECTOR

RONNA VLADIC
PRODUCTION MANAGER

KENNY FELIX
GRAPHIC DESIGNER

LEE PATIN
CONTROLLER

BRENT BRAUN
COMMUNICATIONS DIRECTOR

BOB MATSON
DIRECTOR OF SALES

Introduction

I'd first seen the Teenage Mutant Ninja Turtles in an ad in the pages of the Comics Buyers' Guide. But it took my pal Michael Dooney to introduce them to me. Although I thought it was a funny idea and name, I didn't order it through the mail. Mike, (who I'd gotten to know through the mail when he bought my fanzine Graphic Fantasy) wrote to Eastman and Laird and offered to trade them a copy of his comic book, Gizmo, for one of their books. Pete and Kevin wrote back to Mike, saying that they'd both like a copy and sent him two copies of Teenage Mutant Ninja Turtles #1. Mike then sent one of those to me.

I remember writing to Mike and telling him that, while I thought the comic was cool, I didn't think the creators should continue it— we all got the joke— what more needed to be said?

They showed me.

Dozens of comics and concepts, cartoons and toys, puzzles and games, breakfast cereal and tasty pasta. I'm still waiting for Mike to say "I told you so."

Anyway, years later I got a call from Michael Dooney. He was working at Mirage in some kind of editorial capacity and wondered if I'd like to do a pin up for the fiftieth issue of the Teenage Mutant Ninja Turtles. I said sure.

A year later Mike and I talked about doing some kind of crossover, we'd wanted to work together for some time and, now that Image was up and running and I could basically do as I pleased, the opportunity had presented itself. That conversation lead to the first of two Savage Dragon/TMNT crossovers. My treatment of their characters lead to me being selected to take up the reins and run with the Turtles in a new ongoing series (as Kevin and Pete took a long deserved break).

I put together a crack team of comic book professionals that turned out to be even more capable of producing great Turtle tales then I thought possible. They hit the ground running and were turning out some of the most exciting comics I'd read in ages from the very first panel!

Writer, Gary Carlson, first worked with me in the pages of his comic book Megaton nearly fifteen years ago when we co-created Vanguard. In addition to the Turtles, he's written Vanguard, Supreme and Big Bang Comics for Image Comics and Berzerker, Night Watchmen and more Big Bang Comics for Caliber press.

Penciller, Frank Fosco, worked with Gary before on a feature called Ethrian for Megaton. He also worked on Superman, Steele, Robin and Ground Zero for DC Comics.

Chance Wolf gave me a hand inking the first issue of TMNT and assisted Andrew Pepoy on the second issue. Chance had worked on books from Top Cow, assisted Todd McFarlane inking some Spawn pages and did most every issue of Jim Valentino's ShadowHawk. Andrew Pepoy inked the New ShadowHawk for Image and issues of just about everything for everybody elsewhere. He's one of the hardest working guys in comics and on the side, he writes, pencils and inks his own delightful creations, Simone & Ajax.

Chris Eliopoulos has lettered nearly every comic book to come out of my studio and continues to be the best damned letterer on the planet.

Reuben Rude and IHOC colored the covers and they work with me on The Savage Dragon. I think they're tops!

When I first took on the Turtles, I thought that we could do a good job with them. It wasn't until pages started showing up in my hands to ink that I could see how good. The folks at Mirage have been very supportive and there's not an issue that goes by where I don't say to myself— "I can't believe they're letting us get away with this stuff." Now that the book is going full throttle, I'm floored with just how good it actually is and as much as I'd like to take credit for that, it's all Gary, Frank and Andrew's doing. Them, and a couple of guys who got the ball rolling... named Kevin and Pete.

Erik Larsen

I wasn't a TMNT fan the first time around, in the mid-1980s. I was a superhero junkie, writing and editing my own independent comic book MEGATON, eagerly digging through the piles and piles of other indie comics, looking for pencilers and inkers to work with. My friends all recommended TMNT to me, and I bought the first issue (but not until it went into its second printing) and even then I never gave it a chance. It wasn't superheroes!

However, my son Scott was born at just about the same time as the Turtles, and as he grew older, he was swept up in the TMNT phenomenon that followed. We watched the cartoons, played with the toys (lots and lots of Turtles toys) and went to the movies together. Then he grew up a little, and finally outgrew the Turtles. Me too.

I was skeptical when Erik Larsen told me that he was thinking of publishing a new TMNT comic at Image Comics. He wanted to do a grittier book for kids like my son who had outgrown the TV turtles. I went out and bought all the back issues of the original Mirage series and read them.

And I loved them, especially the Eastman & Laird issues. I finally discovered what all the shouting had been about. There were lots of great characters and concepts to play with. I was hooked.

It's been a great year, working on the TMNT. I hope the stories in this volume are as much fun to read as they were to write. I'd like to thank the gang at Mirage for being so supportive of what we're doing, and especially Peter Laird for his help and great suggestions every month.

Gary Carlson

My strongest recollection of the original Turtles is of drawing sketches of them for my two sons in the early eighties.

When the TMNT phenomenon hit, I was busy working with Gary Carlson who was busy trying to get Megaton comics off the ground. Through Gary I met Erik and little did we know that today, under Erik's direction, we would be doing the Turtles as part of the Image universe.

I'm excited to be the penciller of this book and I am looking forward to continuing to be part of the creative team that takes the Turtles to places they've never been before. So, hang on for the ride.

Frank Fosco

As a kid, I had a lot of fun reading the Turtles starting with the very first issue. Now here I am working on it. I hope some other kid is having as much fun with today's Turtles.

Andrew Pepoy

I'm just a goddam letterer—leave me alone. Aren't there more important people to bother?

Chris Eliopoulos

I laughed, I cried, I gave a big sigh of relief when the first Image comic arrived at Mirage, and on time even. All concerns we may have had when control of the TMNT comic was first turned over to Erik, and Image, vanished. Gary Carlson does a fabulous job constructing interesting, action packed, and humorous stories, and, as can be seen in these first five issues, Frank Fosco and Andrew Pepoy have developed a real feel for black and white art. And, as a bonus, we get to enjoy Erik's great cover art and warped sense of humor in the "Shell Shocked" letters pages. Way to go, guys!!

Gary Richardson, CEO,
Mirage Studios

Erik, Gary, Frank and Andrew, with one broad stroke of glorious black and white, have stripped away the layers, taken the Turtles back to the basics, then reinvented them. With my highest praise and regards; "Guys...you brought the raw, edgy, kick-ass, heart and soul back where it belongs! Thanks!"

Kevin Eastman

Working with Gary Carlson from the "approvals" end of things, here at Mirage Studios, I've had the pleasure of watching the book develop from a slightly tentative start to the exciting, innovative comic it is today. This new iteration of the TMNT has heart, soul...and balls.

Peter Laird

I've been buying the Turtles faithfully for years and I just noticed that there are pictures on the inside of these comics as well! Very cool.

Josh Eichorn

THAT SOUND! IT'S NOT-- FIREWORKS?
NO, MASTER-- IT SOUNDED LIKE GUNFIRE! OH GOD--!
DONNY'S BEEN SHOT! SOMEONE'S GONNA PAY FOR THIS!
JEEZ-- LOOK OUT!
CLINK
GOOD! THEY'RE ALL HERE!
AW FER PETE'S SAKE! WHO INVITED CYBORGS?
THERE'S NOTHING I HATE MORE THAN STINKIN' CYBORGS!
DO YOU RECOGNIZE THEM, LEONARDO?
NO, MASTER SPLINTER--

INCOMING!
BRAKKADOOM!
HAPPY BIRTHDAY, FREAKS! IT'S GONNA BE YOUR LAST ONE!
WHAT'S THE MATTER, SHORTY? NEVER HAD A SURPRISE PARTY BEFORE?
I GOT YOUR PRESENT RIGHT HERE! I DIDN'T HAVE TIME TO WRAP IT! HAW HAW!
ER-- I'M WILLING TO WAIT!
I'VE NEVER SEEN THESE GUYS BEFORE IN MY LIFE!

LET'S SHOW THESE SLIMEBALLS HOW WE DEAL WITH PARTY CRASHERS!
MOVE IT OR LOSE IT, MIKEY!
ARRGH!
SLASH
YOU DIRTY RAT! YOU SHOT MY BRUDDER!
THUAKK
AND NOW FOR MY NEXT IMPRESSION --
MASTER! HOW IS HE--?
DONATELLO APPEARS TO BE IN SHOCK, BUT HIS PULSE IS STRONG. PERHAPS THE SHOTS MISSED HIS MAJOR ORGANS. I WILL DO WHAT I CAN FOR HIM UNTIL YOU AND YOUR BROTHERS DISPOSE OF THE INTRUDERS!
RIGHT! IT'S PARTY TIME!

RAPHAEL! YOU'RE A SITTING DUCK!
CRAP!
GAK! SHOOT HIM, DAMMIT! SHOOT HIM!
NO SWEAT, RAPH!
DON'T YOU KNOW IT'S NOT POLITE TO POINT?
YOU THINK I'M DEFEATED, FOOL? ALREADY MY CYBERNETIC ARMOR HAS CAUTERIZED THE WOUND AND INJECTED PAINKILLERS AND ADRENALIN INTO MY BLOODSTREAM!
I DON'T BELIEVE I'M SEEING THIS!
THEN THE ORGANIC METAL CELLS REPLICATE TO REPLACE THE LOST MASS!
AND FINALLY THE SYMBIOTIC ORGANISM GROWS ME A PROSTHETIC HAND, BASED ON MY OWN DNA--
COMPLETE WITH A NEW PLASMA BLASTER! NOW LET'S SEE HOW TOUGH YOU ARE, TURTLE-BOY!
ULP!

BRAKKA BRAKKA BRAKKA BRAKKA BRAKKA BRAKKA
SLASH!
LET'S SEE YOUR FANCY ARMOR GROW YOU A NEW HEAD, BIG MOUTH!
WHOA! IT IS!
IT'S ACTUALLY CLOSING THE WOUND-- TRYING TO HEAL IT!
YOU KNOW WHAT THEY SAY-- IT WON'T HEAL IF YOU PICK IT!
KRAKK!
ONE-TWO-THREE! AND THE PINHEAD IS DOWN FOR THE COUNT!
NICE WORK, MIKEY: YOU BEAT HIS BRAINS IN!
LET'S KICK SOME MORE CYBORG BUTT FOR DONNY!
STOP!
WHOA! I GET FIRST DIBS ON THAT TUSH!

MAKE ONE MOVE AND YOUR SENSEI DIES!
I TOO AM NINJA, AND WHILE THERE IS NO HONOR IN KILLING A DRUGGED OPPONENT --
I WILL NOT HESITATE TO SLIT HIS MANGY THROAT IF YOU INTERFERE!

CALM DOWN, RAPH! BE PATIENT --THEY'RE ON OUR TURF! WAIT UNTIL THEY MAKE A MISTAKE!
WE'VE GOT WHAT WE CAME FOR: ONE RAT AND ONE TURTLE!
YOU CYBORGS TAKE THE PRISONERS OUT THE WAY WE CAME AND I'LL GUARD YOUR BACKS!
NO! THESE FREAKS SKRAGGED WILSON! I SAY WE EXTERMINATE THEM, PIMIKO! I'M IN CHARGE HERE--DON'T INTERFERE!
THESE "FREAKS" ARE NINJA!
YOU'D BE AS DEAD AS WILSON IF I HADN'T INTERFERED!
YOU WOULDN'T EVEN HAVE GOTTEN PAST THEIR TRAPS AND ALARMS IN THE SEWERS WITHOUT MY INTERFERENCE!
STILL YOU ARE WELCOME TO STAY BEHIND. I WILL EXPLAIN YOUR DEATH TO THE DRAGONLORD!
UH--!
NO--I'M COMING!
YOU THINK THAT WE'RE GONNA JUST LET YOU WALTZ OUT OF HERE? THINK AGAIN, BABE!
THE SECOND YOU TURN YOUR BACK ON ME, I'LL CARVE MY NAME IN YOUR BARE BUTT!

WE WILL CROSS BLADES WHEN WE MEET AGAIN, NINJA TURTLE. YOU HAVE MY WORD! SAVE YOUR MACHO POSTURING 'TIL THEN!
AND JUST TO MAKE CERTAIN--
FASH!
ANOTHER GRENADE!
BUT NOW WE MUST DEPART. ANY ATTEMPT TO FOLLOW WILL RESULT IN THE DEATH OF YOUR FRIENDS!
WE'LL SEE ABOUT THAT!
NO! IT WAS JUST A FLASH BOMB! SHE TRICKED US!
THEY'RE GETTING AWAY!
NO WAY! LET'S GO!
WE'LL HEAD 'EM OFF AT THE PASS!
WHOA, WHAT A BABE! DID YOU SEE THOSE LEGS?
SO WHAT? SHE'S A DOG! WOOF WOOF!
A DOG? ARE YOU CRAZY, RAPH?
WHY ELSE WOULD SHE WEAR A BAG OVER HER HEAD?
THERE'S NO SIGN OF ANYBODY OUT HERE, I'LL CLIMB THAT PHONE POLE AND TAKE A LOOK AROUND!
WAIT! THAT SOUND-- SOME KIND OF MOTOR!

AW, NUTS-- A HELICOPTER! WE'LL NEVER CATCH THEM NOW!
WE COULD'VE TAKEN THOSE BUMS EASY! NICE GOING, LEO!
ADIOS, FREAKOS!
SECURE THE PRISONERS, JACKSON. THEY ARE STILL EXTREMELY DANGEROUS!
YOU WORRY TOO MUCH, PIMIKO!
"WAIT 'TIL THEY MAKE A MISTAKE!" NOW WHAT, FEARLESS LEADER?
SHUT UP, RAPH!
THE RAT IS STILL IN DREAMLAND, BUT I THINK THAT THE TURTLE HAS BLED TO DEATH! HE'S NOT MOVING.
ALIVE OR DEAD --NO MATTER. AN AUTOPSY WILL SERVE THE DRAGONLORD'S PURPOSE!
NICE BIRTHDAY, FREAK.
HAPPY BIRTHDAY!!
HAPPY
MASTER--?

HAPPY BIRTHDAY, MY SONS.
EIGHTEEN YEARS AGO TODAY, A CANISTER OF RADIOACTIVE WASTE CHANGED ALL OF OUR LIVES.
I SAID NO STUPID HATS!
AS YOU KNOW, I LIVED A LONG LIFE AS A NORMAL RAT BEFORE THE MUTAGEN TRANSFORMED ME. NOW, EVEN MY HUMAN LIFESPAN NEARS AN END.
I AM OLD AND VERY WEARY.
PARTY POOPER.
SHHH!
SOON, I SHALL BE GONE.
AW, YOU'VE BEEN THREATENING TO CROAK ON US EVER SINCE I CAN REMEMBER, MASTER.
NO PARENT WISHES TO OUTLIVE HIS CHILDREN. I WILL GO HAPPILY WHEN MY TIME EXPIRES.
BUT I WORRY. I KNOW YOU OFTEN FEEL ALIENATED-- THAT YOU FEAR THERE IS NO PLACE FOR YOU IN THIS WORLD.
YEAH. YOU'LL OUTLIVE US ALL, SPLINTER!
OF ALL MY ACCOMPLISHMENTS, I TAKE THE MOST PRIDE IN YOU FOUR, BOTH AS SENSEI AND FATHER.
YOUR LIVES WILL BE WHAT YOU MAKE OF THEM. MY GIFT TO YOU TODAY IS A VIEW OF A LIFE THAT COULD HAVE BEEN--
BEHOLD, YOUR LIVES-- UNTOUCHED BY MUTAGEN!

YOU'RE SAYING WE SHOULD BE THANKFUL FOR WHAT WE'VE GOT, MASTER?
FOUR TURTLES IN A BOWL! JUST LIKE US WHEN SPLINTER FOUND US!
HEH! THEY'RE CUTE!
YES, DONATELLO! YOU SOMETIMES WISH TO FIT INTO MAN'S WORLD. BUT NEVER FORGET THAT THIS IS THE LIFE YOU WERE BORN TO, AND HOW FAR YOU'VE RISEN ABOVE IT!
I DISCOVERED THESE FOUR FELLOWS IN THE SEWER YESTERDAY, NO DOUBT ABANDONED BY A BORED OWNER.
THIS COULD HAVE BEEN YOUR DESTINY. WHICH EXISTENCE WOULD YOU TRULY PREFER?
I SAVED THE BEST SURPRISE FOR LAST: I BAKED YOU A BIRTHDAY CAKE!
UGH! ANOTHER OF HIS PATENTED "HAIRBALL SPECIALS"!
IF YOU GUYS ARE SMART, YOU'LL STICK TO YOUR FLIES!
DONATELLO-- WOULD YOU PLEASE BRING THE CAKE FROM THE KITCHEN?
THWAKK
OW!
WOW! NICE GUNS! UM-- ARE YOU GUYS PART OF THE SURPRISE?
HAPPY BIRTHDAY, FREAK!

BLAM BLAM BLAM BLAM BLAM BLAM BLAM BLAM BLAM BLAM BLAM BLAM
GAAAA!
YOU CREEPS SHOT ME!
THE TURTLE IS ALIVE AFTER ALL, PIMIKO!
ALIVE AND KICKING, BOZO!
WHOMP
SWAK
SO DISORIENTED! SPLINTER?!! IS HE DEAD? WE'VE GOT TO ESCAPE!
I'M TRYING, BUT IT'S GOT MY GUN!
FOOL! STOP HIM!
THESE CYBORGS ARE WORSE THAN USELESS! IF THAT TURTLE GAINS CONTROL, ALL IS LOST!
THE RAT MUST NOT BE ALLOWED TO ESCAPE! LUCKILY, THERE ARE THREE OTHER TURTLES--

"THAT MAKES THIS ONE EXPENDABLE!"
SKRRASSHH!
PIMIKO! FOR GOD'S SAKE! NO!
OH JEEZ--A HELICOPTER!
IS IT TOO LATE TO CHANGE MY MIND ABOUT ESCAPING?

PWUPWUPWUP!
HELLLLLP!
HEY, STUPID!
DOESN'T THAT ARMOR COME EQUIPPED WITH BOOT JETS OR A ROCKET PACK?
GLIDER WINGS? A PARACHUTE?
AN AIR BAG? OR TWO?
IF IT DOES, FREAK--
-- I DON'T KNOW HOW TO WORK IT!
CRAP!
THIS IS DEFINITELY GOING TO HURT!

NOW WHAT? HOW CAN WE RESCUE SPLINTER AND DONATELLO IF WE DON'T EVEN KNOW WHO SNATCHED THEM?
MAYBE THE HEADLESS HORSEMAN HERE CAN PROVIDE SOME CLUES.
TOO BAD DONATELLO'S NOT HERE. HE WOULD'VE ENJOYED TAKING A CAN OPENER TO THAT ARMORED CORPSE.
ARMOR: YES! CORPSE: NO!
HUH?
THIS GUY ISN'T DEAD! THE ARMOR IS KEEPING HIM ALIVE FOR SOME REASON; HE'S ON LIFE SUPPORT!
THAT'S GROSS! THE POOR GUY IS BRAIN-DEAD!
BRAIN-DEAD? LEO, THE DUDE IS BRAIN-LESS!
HIS HEAD IS ON THE TABLE OVER THERE, FOR CRYIN' OUT LOUD!
WHAT DO WE DO NOW?
WE PUT THIS POOR S.O.B. OUT OF HIS MISERY! CALLING DR. HOWARD, DR. FINE, DR. HOWARD!
AND JUST CALL ME DR. KREVORKIAN!

DANGER! DANGER! HOST ORGANISM IS IMPERILED!
UH-- GUYS?
RAPH? THE ARMOR IS TALKING!
ALL THE MORE REASON TO PULL THE PLUG!
WARNING: DEFENSE MECHANISMS HAVE BEEN ARMED! CEASE ALL HOSTILITIES.
ANY FURTHER ATTEMPTS TO NULLIFY BASE LIFE FORM WILL BE MET WITH EXTREME VIOLENCE!
THE ARMOR MUST BE SOME SORT OF PARASITE! IF YOU KILL THE HOST, THE ARMOR DIES TOO, AND IT DOESN'T WANT TO GO PEACEFULLY!
WHAT'S IT GONNA DO-- BITE ME? HA HA!
ADIOS, AMOEBA!
KLIK
FWA-BOOSH!

NO FAIR! IT BLASTED RAPH BY REMOTE CONTROL!
KA-CHANG
AARGH!
SHRAKK
YOU JUST SHOT YOUR LAST WAD, WHATEVER YOU ARE! MEET MY KATANA--
SLASH!
SHWIIING
IT SLICES--IT DICES--
IT CUTS THROUGH TIN CANS--
CHOPCHOPCHOPC
CHOPCHOPCHOPC
CHOPCHOPCHOPC
CHOPCHOPCHOPC
AND IT'S STILL SHARP ENOUGH TO MAKE COLE SLAW!
REST IN PIECES, CREEP!
WHUDD!

RAPH, ARE YOU OKAY?
I DON'T KNOW! IT FRIED MY FACE!
IT HURTS, LEO! IT HURTS BAD!
AND I CAN'T SEE VERY WELL!
HOW DOES IT LOOK?
YOU PROBABLY WON'T BE VOTED THE "WORLD'S SEXIEST MAN" THIS YEAR, RAPHAEL.
C'MON. THERE'S SALVE AND BANDAGES IN THE FIRST AID KIT!
WHAT IN THE--?
MASTER SPLINTER--? BUT HOW--?
HUSH, LEONARDO AND LISTEN!
I WAS DRUGGED. MY BODY AND CONSCIOUS MIND ARE COMATOSE.
FORTUNATELY, IT IS SIMILAR TO THE SPIRITUAL STATE I ACHEIVE DURING MEDITATION AND MY SOUL-SELF WAS ABLE TO ESCAPE TO THE ASTRAL PLANE.

MY CAPTORS ARE TRAVELING NORTH AND WEST, AND THE TERRAIN BELOW IS HILLY AND WOODED. YOUR BROTHER DONATELLO NO LONGER ACCOMPANIES US.
HE ESCAPED SOON AFTER THE HELICOPTER TOOK. HE EXPERIENCED GREAT PAIN AND I LOST TRACK OF HIM.
PIMIKO. LOOK! THE RAT IS FLOATING!
INCREDIBLE! HE MUST BE AT LEAST A SEVENTH LEVEL NINJA TO ACCOMPLISH THAT TRICK!
UNFORTUNATELY, I HAVE BEEN DISCOVERED. I SHALL ATTEMPT TO CONTACT YOU LATER.
HIS SOUL-SELF IS ROAMING THE ASTRAL PLANE! STOP HIM!
YOU HEARD THE LADY, RAT-MAN--
LIGHTS OUT!
FAREWELL, MY SON.
FARE--
MASTER!!
HE'S GONE!

MY NAME IS DONATELLO. I AM NINJA!
I DON'T KNOW WHO THE TIN MAN HERE IS, BUT HE'S DEFINITELY LACKING IN THE HEART DEPARTMENT.
HE AND HIS CYBORG BUDDIES HAVE BEEN TRYING TO KILL ME SINCE LAST NIGHT--
--WHEN THEY USED ME FOR TARGET PRACTICE AT MY HOME IN THE SEWERS!
YOU'RE DEAD MEAT, TURTLE!

OF COURSE, IF HE DOESN'T KILL ME, THE FALL PROBABLY WILL!
YOU PUSHED US OUT OF THE HELICOPTER, YA STOOPID FREAKIN' REPTILE --
I'M GONNA AT LEAST HAVE THE SATISFACTION OF SEEIN' YOU DIE FIRST!
NOT IF I CAN HELP IT.
BLAM!
I HAVE TO ADMIT, HE HAD MORE BRAINS THAN I GAVE HIM CREDIT FOR!

OOPS!
THE MORON'S GUN WENT OFF!
HE WENT FROM SHOOTING HIS MOUTH OFF TO SHOOTING HIS OWN HEAD OFF!
AT LEAST I CAN CONCENTRATE ON TRYING TO STAY ALIVE NOW, MAYBE I CAN FIND SOMETHING SOFT TO LAND ON--
LIKE A PILE OF FOAM RUBBER OR A TRUCKFUL OF FEATHERS OR MAYBE A SWIMMING POOL!
THERE'S ONLY ONE PROBLEM--
CAN'T BREATHE--GOT TO STAY AWAKE!
GOT TO--

UPSTATE, NEW YORK...
WAS THIS RAT REALLY FLOATING, PIMIKO?
IT'S CALLED LEVITATING.
AND YES, HE WAS. I WOULD HAVE USED A STRONGER DRUG ON HIM HAD I TRULY BELIEVED HE WAS A NINJA MASTER.
PREPARE TO LAND.
THE DRAGONLORD IS IN THE LABORATORY, LADY PIMIKO.
I AM NOT A LADY.
I AM A WARRIOR! I AM NINJA!
INFORM LORD KOMODO OF OUR RETURN! I SHALL JOIN HIM SHORTLY.

FIRST WE SHALL SEE TO OUR GUEST'S ACCOMMODATIONS.
ACTUALLY, THIS CELL MAY BE MORE SANITARY THAN THE SEWER WE TOOK THE RODENT FROM!
A CHILLING VOICE FLOATS FROM THE DEPTHS OF THE NEXT CELL: "HEY, BABE! HOW ABOUT PARKING THAT RAT IN HERE WITH ME?"
AFTER TWO DAYS OF BREAD AND SOUP, EVEN A SCRAWNY RAT WILL TASTE LIKE FILET MIGNON!
LISTEN YOU--SHUT THAT BIG MOUTH OF YOURS--
OR I'LL SHUT IT FOR YOU!
CHOMP
ULP!

FOOL!
OW OW OW! HE BIT MY HAND OFF!
METAL? PTOOEY! I HATE STINKIN' CYBORGS!
THAT ORGANIC NANO-CIRCUITRY WILL GROW BACK, BUT IT STILL HURTS LIKE HELL!
LET'S SEE YOU TRY THAT WITH NO TEETH, JERK!
LEAVE HIM! THE DRAGONLORD PREFERS HIS TEST SUBJECTS ALIVE!
YEAH? HE PREFERS EVERYBODY ALIVE EXCEPT FOR ME AND MY PARTNERS!
AND THEY'RE DEAD BECAUSE THEY FOLLOWED YOUR ORDERS!
I'M SICK OF YOU AND YOUR ORDERS, PIMIKO!
GAK!
AND I AM TIRED OF ISSUING ORDERS THAT ARE DISOBEYED!
YOU MAY REJOIN YOUR COMRADES! YOUR SERVICES HAVE BEEN TERMINATED!
I SHALL INFORM THE DRAGONLORD OF YOUR DECISION.

YOU BITCH! YOU THINK THAT PUNY SWORD OF YOURS WILL STOP ME? MY ARMOR IS HEALING THE WOUND ALREADY--
YOU THERE, IN THE CAGE-- MAKO?
THERE IS FRESH MEAT SOMEWHERE INSIDE ALL OF THAT METAL! IT IS YOURS IF YOU WANT IT!
THANKS, BABE! JUST LIKE EATING SPAM OUT OF THE CAN!
YOU WILL PAY FOR THIS, PIMIKO! I SWEAR IT!

I DON'T LIKE RUNNING AWAY, LEO!
WE SHOULD'VE STAYED AND WAITED FOR THEM TO SHOW UP AGAIN!
JEEZ, RAPH-- THEY WALKED IN, SHOT DONNY FULL OF HOLES AND KIDNAPPED BOTH HIM AND SPLINTER!
AW, WE KICKED THOSE CYBORG'S BUTTS ALL OVER THE PLACE!
YEAH, BUT THAT NINJA BABE WAS GOOD.
TOO GOOD! AND SHE PROMISED TO COME BACK WITH REINFORCEMENTS! SHE WON'T CATCH US UNPREPARED AGAIN!
HOW MUCH FARTHER, LEO? THIS STUFF WEIGHS A TON!
WE'RE THERE, MIKEY!

THERE'S RUNNING WATER, INDOOR PLUMBING, LIVE ELECTRICITY, AND A PHONE LINE WAITING TO BE CONNECTED.
BEST OF ALL, IT'S DESERTED. NOBODY COMES HERE ANYMORE!
THIS IS GREAT, LEO! LOOK AT ALL THE STORAGE!
WHAT IS THIS PLACE?
IT'S THE MAUSOLEUM VAULT IN WESTWOOD CEMETERY. THEY USED TO STORE CASKETS IN HERE DURING THE WINTER.
M-M-MAUSOLEUM?
HE MEANS A MORGUE, STUPID!
BOOGA-BOOGA!
GAAAA!
SLAM
GAK
CHILL OUT, MIKEY! IT'S ME-- RAPHAEL! IT WAS ONLY A JOKE!

HARDY HAR HAR! REAL FUNNY! THOSE STUPID BANDAGES MAKE YOU LOOK LIKE A *MUMMY*!
YOU'RE THE GUY THAT BANDAGED ME UP AFTER THE CYBORGS FRIED MY FACE, MIKE!
HEY, LEO!
OH YEAH, HEH HEH!
THIS *IS* A GREAT PLACE!
BUT WHAT DO WE DO NOW, FEARLESS LEADER? SIT ON OUR HANDS ?
NOPE. WE'VE GOT TO FIND OUT WHO THIS *DRAGONLORD* GUY IS AND RESCUE DON AND SPLINTER!
MIKE WILL SEE WHAT HE CAN FIND OUT VIA THE INTERNET USING DON'S COMPUTER.
I'D LIKE YOU TO CHECK WITH YOUR CONTACTS IN THE *FOOT* CLAN. THAT BABE WAS NINJA.
THE FOOT MIGHT KNOW SOMETHING ABOUT PIMIKO OR HER BOSS! WHY IS HER NAME SO *FAMILIAR*?
PIMIKO: A SORCERESS WHO RULED FEUDAL JAPAN WITH THE AID OF ONE THOUSAND WOMEN AND ONLY ONE MAN! I LOOKED IT UP!

I'LL LEAVE THIS WAY. I'VE GOT JUST THE MUG TO HAUNT A GRAVEYARD WITH!
HOLD ON, RAPH, I'VE GOT SOMETHING FOR YOU--
-- TO HELP PROTECT YOUR FACE!
COOL! ONE OF CASEY'S OLD MASKS!
HOW DO I LOOK ?
IT'S A MAJOR IMPROVEMENT!
THANKS. I THINK! SEE YOU LATER, LEO!
BE CAREFUL. AND MAKE SURE YOU'RE NOT FOLLOWED BACK HERE!
DON'T WORRY. I'LL MELT INTO THE SHADOWS AND BECOME INVISIBLE! NO ONE WILL EVEN KNOW I'M OUT AND ABOUT!
PIMIKO-- THIS IS ANGEL, I'M STILL BABYSITTING THE LITTLE BOYS.
THEY HAVE A NEW CLUBHOUSE. HERE ARE THE DIRECTIONS--

THAT'S GREAT, ANGEL. I'LL CALL THE GIRLS AND WE'LL HELP YOU RAID THEIR ICEBOX.
HAVE THE FUNDING ON THE CYBORG PROJECT CANCELLED.
ATRIFICIAL INTELLIGENCE, MY EYE! DIMIKO SAYS THEY WERE THE DUMBEST, MOST WORTHLESS WARRIORS SHE'S EVER SEEN!
YES SIR.
HIS PULSE IS ACCELERATING AGAIN. MORE ANESTHETIC!
WARLORD KOMODO! WE'VE CONCLUDED THE PRELIMINARY TESTS, AND ALL INDICATIONS ARE THAT THE SUBJECT IS DEFINITELY *NOT* AN *ANTHROPOMORPH*!
DESPITE THIS PERSON'S PHYSICAL ATTRIBUTES, AND THE FACT THAT HE REFERS TO HIMSELF AS "THE *WEASEL*
THERE IS ZERO PERCENT ANIMAL DNA IN HIS CELLULAR STRUCTURE.
YOUR "WEASEL" IS MERELY A MUTANT OF SOME SORT--
--AND NOT THE *HYBRID* YOU ARE SEEKING!

THEN HE IS OF NO FURTHER USE TO ME! RELEASE HIM.
THE SUBJECT HAS AMAZING RECUPERATIVE AND HEALING ABILITIES THAT COULD BENEFIT ALL OF MANKIND! I'D LIKE TO STUDY HIM FURTHER?
THE WELFARE OF THIS BEAST IS OF NO CONCERN TO ME.
BUT STUDY HIM ON YOUR OWN TIME, DOCTOR!
?
DOCTOR! THE PATIENT'S VITAL SIGNS ARE RACING!
SNIKT
IT'S AWAKE!
GRRRR
SKRASH!
IT'S TRYING TO FREE ITSELF! TRANQUILIZE IT NOW!
TOO LATE! THE ANIMAL HAS BROKEN LOOSE!

ANIMAL?
YOUR PEOPLE STALKED ME, ATTACKED ME, DOPED ME UP, CUT ME OPEN AND JUST NOW YOU SIGNED MY DEATH WARRANT!
I'M NOT THE ANIMAL HERE, BUBBA!
UNFORTUNATELY NOT, MR. WEASEL.
SLASH!!
GAK
AND THAT FACT MAKES YOU EXTREMELY EXPENDABLE!
THANK YOU, PIMIKO!
I EXIST ONLY TO SERVE YOU, DRAGONLORD! AND NOW I MUST BE LEAVING!
MY KUNOICHI HAVE LOCATED THE TURTLES.
GOOD! I EXPECT YOU TO BRING ONE BACK THIS TIME.

ANY LUCK, MIKEY?
NOTHING ON THE DRAGONLORD GUY, BUT LOTS OF NEW CHEESECAKE PIX OF TERI HATCHER!
WHERE'S "NUMBER ONE SON"?
LEO'S OVER THERE. MEDITATING.
HE'S TRYING TO REESTABLISH MENTAL CONTACT WITH SPLINTER!
OH BROTHER. EMPHASIS ON THE MENTAL!
SPLINTER?
PLEASE CONTACT ME AGAIN, MASTER!
LEONARDO!
MASTER SPLINTER-- IS THAT YOU?
SORRY, BUT I CAN'T TAKE YOUR CALL RIGHT NOW, SO PLEASE LEAVE A MESSAGE AFTER THE BEEP.
WHAT THE--?

REAL FUNNY, YOU JERKS! I'LL NEVER REACH THE ASTRAL PLANE IF YOU WON'T LET ME CONCENTRATE!
HA HA HA
HA HA HA
EVEN ZILLIONTH LEVEL NINJA AND ZEN MASTERS HAVE TROUBLE ACHIEVING THOUGHT PROJECTION! YOU'RE WASTING YOUR TIME, LEO!
GO AHEAD AND LAUGH! SPLINTER CONTACTED ME THAT WAY!
AND IF HE TRIES AGAIN, AT LEAST ONE OF US WILL BE READY TO HELP HIM!
OKAY, OKAY! I'LL TELL MIKEY WHAT MY CONTACTS WITH THE FOOT CLAN HAD TO SAY!
FINE! JUST LEAVE ME ALONE!
HAPPY TRAILS, COSMIC COWBOY.

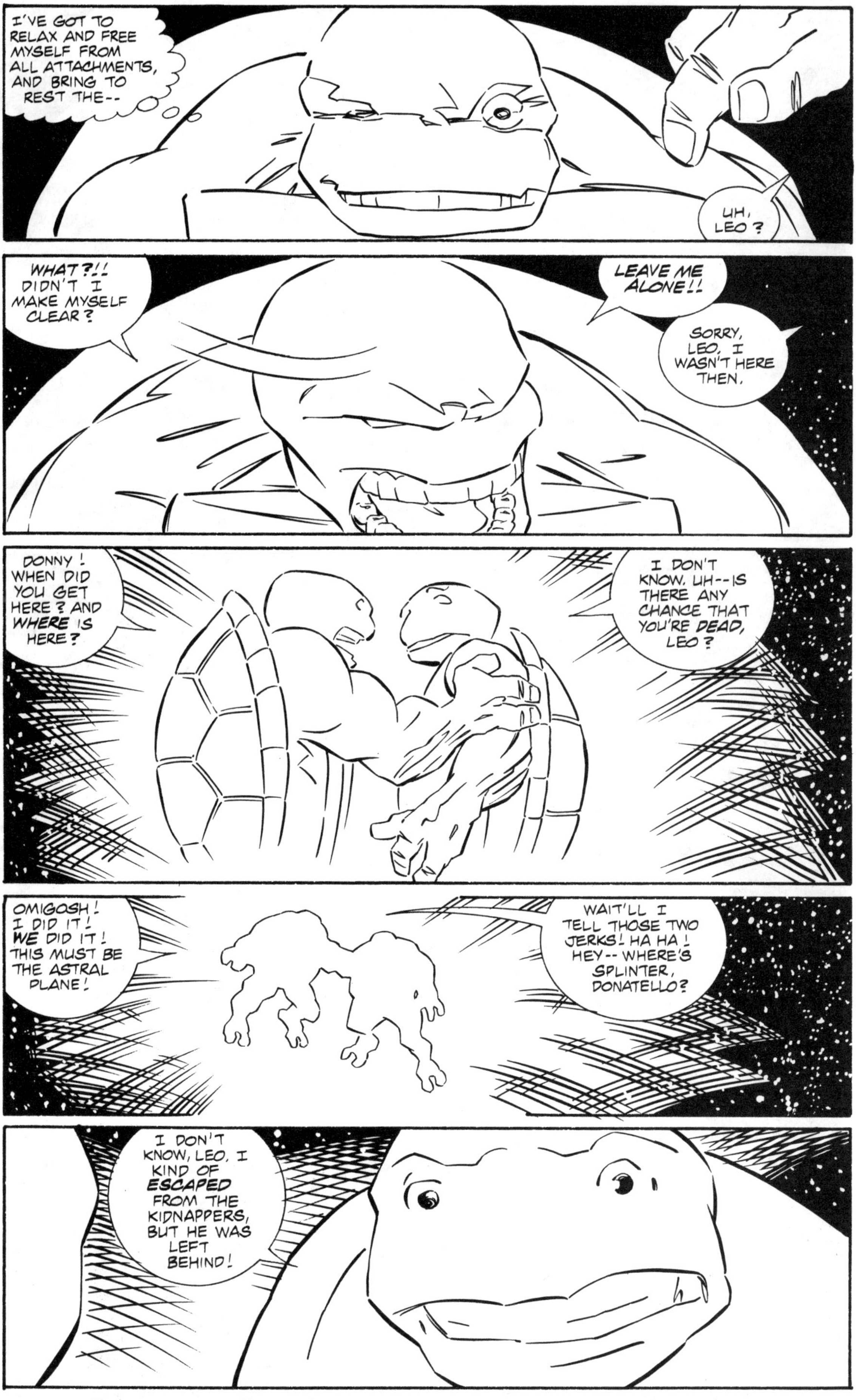

I'VE GOT TO RELAX AND FREE MYSELF FROM ALL ATTACHMENTS, AND BRING TO REST THE--
UH, LEO?
WHAT?!! DIDN'T I MAKE MYSELF CLEAR?
LEAVE ME ALONE!!
SORRY, LEO, I WASN'T HERE THEN.
DONNY! WHEN DID YOU GET HERE? AND WHERE IS HERE?
I DON'T KNOW. UH--IS THERE ANY CHANCE THAT YOU'RE DEAD, LEO?
OMIGOSH! I DID IT! WE DID IT! THIS MUST BE THE ASTRAL PLANE!
WAIT'LL I TELL THOSE TWO JERKS! HA HA! HEY-- WHERE'S SPLINTER, DONATELLO?
I DON'T KNOW, LEO, I KIND OF ESCAPED FROM THE KIDNAPPERS, BUT HE WAS LEFT BEHIND!

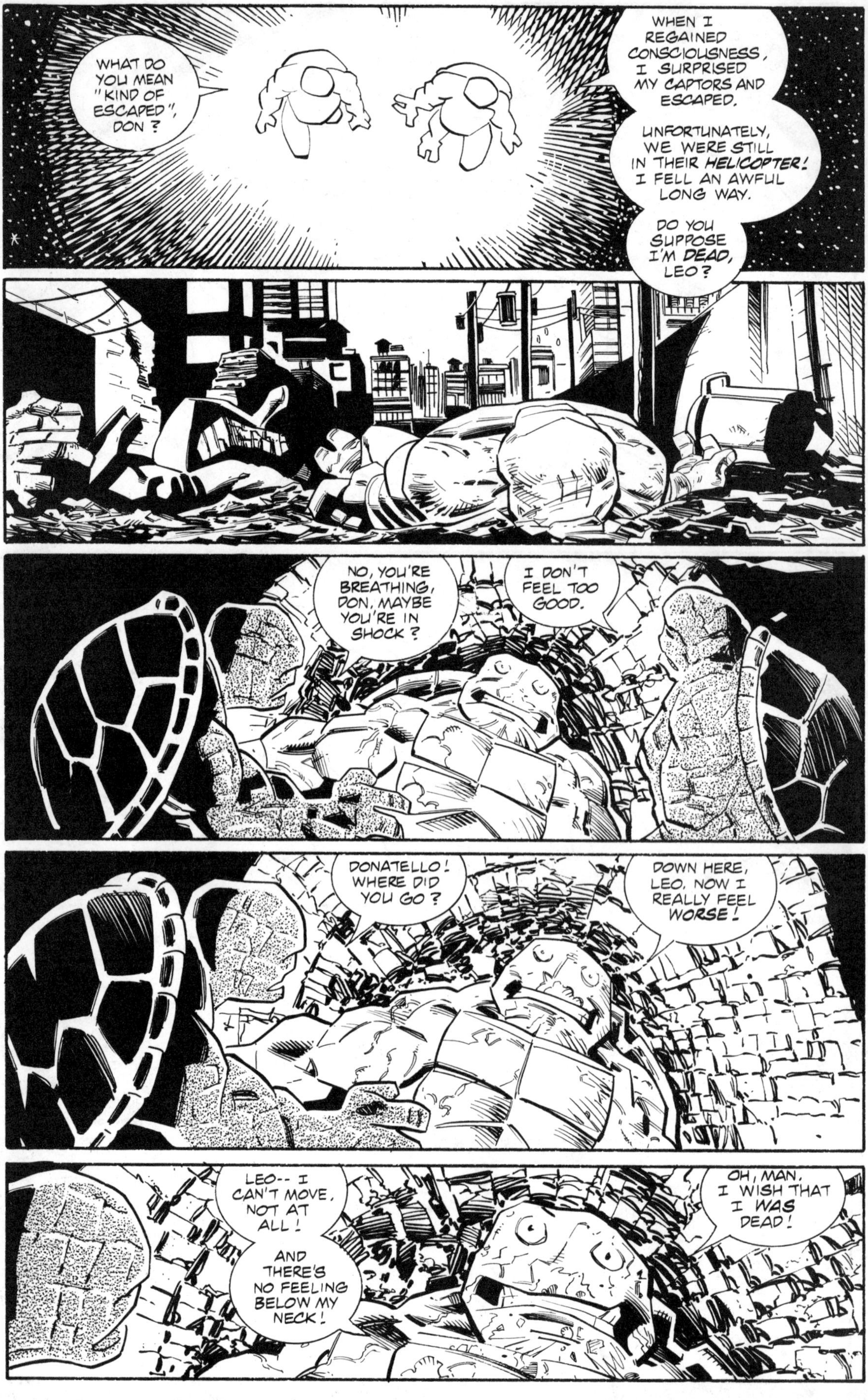
WHAT DO YOU MEAN "KIND OF ESCAPED", DON ?
WHEN I REGAINED CONSCIOUSNESS, I SURPRISED MY CAPTORS AND ESCAPED.
UNFORTUNATELY, WE WERE STILL IN THEIR HELICOPTER! I FELL AN AWFUL LONG WAY.
DO YOU SUPPOSE I'M DEAD, LEO ?
NO, YOU'RE BREATHING, DON. MAYBE YOU'RE IN SHOCK ?
I DON'T FEEL TOO GOOD.
DONATELLO! WHERE DID YOU GO ?
DOWN HERE, LEO. NOW I REALLY FEEL WORSE!
LEO-- I CAN'T MOVE, NOT AT ALL!
AND THERE'S NO FEELING BELOW MY NECK!
OH, MAN. I WISH THAT I WAS DEAD!

HERE'S THREE HUNDRED ACRES OF PROPERTY IN UPSTATE NEW YORK OWNED BY A SUBSIDIARY OF KOMODO INC.!
BINGO! THE FOOT CLAN SAID THAT A NINJA BABE NAMED PIMIKO WORKED FOR KOMODO INDUSTRIES!
NAP TIME'S OVER, LEO. WE'VE PINPOINTED THE DRAGONLORD'S HQ, AND IT'S RIGHT ABOUT WERE SPLINTER TOLD YOU IT WAS!
LET'S KICK SOME BUTT!
LEO?
QUIT CLOWNING, LEO, WE'RE SORRY WE GAVE YOU A HARD TIME.
I DON'T THINK HE'S KIDDING. HE'S IN A DEEP TRANCE!
THOK
THOK
THOK
THOK
EYOW! MY BACK!!
SHURIKEN!
AW, NUTS!
I SEE IT BUT I DON'T BELIEVE IT!

THE NINJA BABES--
THEY FOUND US!
PSSST! WAKE UP, LEO! NOW, LEO! PLEASE, LEO?

ON THE CONTRARY, MY YOUNG REPTILES, WE'VE NEVER LOST YOU!
MY KUNOICHI HAVE HAD YOU UNDER CONSTANT SURVEILLANCE SINCE OUR PREVIOUS MEETING.
AND UNFORTUNATELY, I HAVE BEEN ORDERED TO ENSURE THAT THIS MEETING WILL BE OUR LAST!
GET THEM!

YOU'RE WASTING YOUR TIME PRAYING, RATBOY! THERE'S BEEN A PARADE OF FREAKS LIKE YOU 'N ME THROUGH THESE CELLS--
--AND ONCE THEY'RE TAKEN AWAY, THEY NEVER EVER COME BACK! ARE YOU LISTENING TO ME?
THIS PLACE IS THE INHUMANE SOCIETY AND THEY'RE GONNA PUT US TO SLEEP! WE'VE GOT TO ESCAPE!
YOU'RE SCRAWNY--SEE IF YOU CAN SQUEEZE BETWEEN THE BARS! HEY, RATFINK--
QUIT IGNORING ME!!
I AM NOT PRAYING, MAKO. IF YOU WILL SIMPLY BE QUIET AND ALLOW ME TO CONCENTRATE--
AMAZING. HE'S FALLEN ASLEEP!
PERHAPS NOW I CAN CONCENTRATE AND REACH MY SONS BY WAY OF THE ASTRAL PLANE!
ZZZZZ
MUST EMPTY MY MIND--MAKE IT RECEPTIVE WHILE CASTING MY THOUGHTS OUT INTO THE GREAT RIVER--
MUST FREE--MY SOUL--
FROM MY--
ZZZZZ
THE TRANQUILIZER HAS TAKEN EFFECT. TAKE THE RAT TO THE LABORATORY! LORD KOMODO IS INTRIGUED WITH THIS ONE!

MIKE-- KEEP TRYING TO WAKE LEO UP! THESE KUNOICHI NINJA BABES OUTNUMBER US FIVE TO ONE: GREAT ODDS FOR A DANCE, BUT NOT FOR A FIGHT!
IT'S NO USE, RAPH: HE'S IN NEVER-NEVER LAND!
I STILL CAN'T BELIEVE THAT LEO'S SOUL IS OUT SURFING THE ASTRAL PLANE!
LEO! WAKE UP FOR CRYIN' OUT LOUD--
--OR YOU WON'T HAVE A BODY TO WAKE UP IN!
WHERE ARE YOU, LEO?

MEANWHILE, 20 OR SO BLOCKS AWAY...
OH MAN, DONATELLO, ARE YOU EVER IN BAD SHAPE: SHOT FULL OF BULLETS AND THEN DROPPED OUT OF A HELICOPTER!
YOU'RE LUCKY TO BE ALIVE -- AND UNCONSCIOUS!
BUT YOUR SHELL -- IT'S SMASHED LIKE A PUMPKIN! OUCH!
MOAN
COUGH HACK
LEO ?
OVER HERE, DON! THIS CYBORG YOU WERE FIGHTING IS IN WORSE SHAPE THAN YOU!
I THINK HE'S DEAD.
LEO ? WHERE ARE YOU ?

EASY, DONNY. I'M JUST OVER HERE!
HE'S NOT HERE!
I'M RIGHT HERE. YOOHOO! SEE?
IT MUST'VE BEEN A DREAM!
NO! YOU HAD AN OUT OF BODY EXPERIENCE AND BROUGHT ME HERE VIA THE ASTRAL PLANE!
BUT I'M A PHANTOM! YOU CAN'T SEE ME ANYMORE, CAN YOU?
I'M NO USE TO YOU THIS WAY!
I'LL GO GET THE GUYS!
I'LL BE RIGHT BACK, DONATELLO.
YOU OUGHT TO BE SAFE IN THAT DESERTED ALLEY!
I-- I CAN'T MOVE!
IT WASN'T A DREAM! I AM PARALYZED!

OH NO-- I'M LOST! I DON'T KNOW HOW TO FIND MY WAY BACK HOME!
WHAT THE--? LET GO!
RELAX, MY SON. YOU ARE IN GOOD HANDS.
MASTER SPLINTER?
THE ASTRAL PLANE IS A DANGEROUS PLACE FOR ONE WHO HASN'T MASTERED THE NECESSARY SKILLS, LEONARDO!
YOU ARE LUCKY IT WAS I WHO HEARD YOUR FEARS!
DONATELLO IS BADLY CRIPPLED AND HE MAY BE DYING! YOU MUST COME AND HELP HIM, MASTER!
I CAN NOT HELP, MY SON.
I AM A PRISONER. EVEN NOW MY CONCENTRATION FAILS. YOU AND YOUR BROTHERS MUST SUFFICE!
THE BEST I CAN DO IS TO GUIDE YOU HOME. FAREWELL!
MASTER-- WAIT!

FAREWELL.
THE SUBJECTS ABNORMAL BRAIN ACTIVITY HAS SUBSIDED. WE CAN NOW CONCLUDE THIS EXAMINATION.
THE SUBJECT IS A MUTANT. ITS CORE DNA AND CELL STRUCTURE MATCH EXACTLY WITH FILE REFERENCE OF *RATTUS NORVEGICUS*, ALTHOUGH THERE ARE VAGUE OVERTONES OF HUMAN TRAITS.
THERE ARE TRACE AMOUNTS OF *RADIATION* IN THE BLOODSTREAM. IT IS POSSIBLY THE REMNANTS OF THE *MUTAGEN* WHICH CAUSED THE TRANSFORMATION.
WE'RE DRAWING EXTRA BLOOD AND CELL TISSUE TO STUDY.
EXCELLENT! PERHAPS MY SEARCH HAS FINALLY BORE FRUIT!
BRING THE PATIENT TO ME AFTER IT RECOVERS!

IT'S NO USE!
I CAN'T FEEL OR MOVE ANYTHING BELOW MY CHIN!
WHAT'S THAT?
A NOISE! IS SOMEONE THERE?
HELLO!
I'VE FALLEN AND I CAN'T GET UP!
HEH HEH. SOB
SQUEE
ULPS!
A RAT!
SHOO! SCAT!
GET LOST OR I'LL BITE YOU IN HALF!
PHEW. IT'S GONE!
OR IS IT?
IT COULD BE NIBBLING ON MY FINGERS OR TOES--
AND I'D NEVER KNOW!!

I AM WARLORD GO-KOMODO, HEIR TO THE IMPERIAL **DRAGON BUSHIDO** SPIRIT. MY ANCESTORS RULED JAPAN AND I SEEK TO RECLAIM MY THRONE.
YOUR NAMESAKE PETS ARE MAGNIFICENT. ARE THEY TAME?
THE DRAGONS ARE MY **BROTHERS,** NOT PETS AND ARE IN NO WAY DOMESTICATED.
IT'S A GREAT HONOR TO MEET ONE OF SUCH EXALTED LINEAGE.
IT WAS RUMORED THAT THE HOUSE OF KOMODO HAD BEEN EXTERMINATED DURING WORLD WAR I.
MY NAME IS SPLINTER, AND I AM BUT A HUMBLE NINJA.
A *NINJA,* GRANDFATHER RAT?
FORGIVE MY SKEPTICISM, BUT YOU SHALL HAVE TO CONVINCE ME.
THESE TWO ARE SAMURAI!
AS YOU WISH.

SURELY YOU DIDN'T WISH FOR ME TO KILL THEM?
IT WOULD BE SUCH A WASTE.
LET THEM LIVE. THEY ARE-- WERE--AMONG MY ELITE GUARD.
YOU HAVE BEEN TREATED HARSHLY, GRANDFATHER RODENT.
PLEASE ACCEPT MY HUMBLE APOLOGIES AND BE WELCOME AS AN HONORED GUEST IN MY CASTLE.
AND NOW WILL SATISFY MY CURIOSITY AND EXPLAIN HOW A NINJA CAME TO BE TRANSFORMED INTO A RAT?
I FEAR I CANNOT TELL YOU THAT.
BUT I CAN TELL YOU THE TALE OF HOW A RAT BECAME NINJA!

"MY TALE BEGINS IN JAPAN, WHERE I WAS THE PET OF HAMATO YOSHI, GREATEST WARRIOR OF THE DREADED FOOT CLAN."
"IT AMUSED HIM THAT I MIMICKED HIS MOVEMENTS AS HE PRACTICED NINJITSU."
"MY MASTER KILLED A RIVAL DEFENDING THE HONOR OF THE WOMAN HE LOVED AND WAS FORCED TO FLEE FOR HIS LIFE."
"MY MASTER TOOK HIS BRIDE AND A FEW CHOICE BELONGINGS INCLUDING MYSELF AND STARTED A NEW LIFE---"
"IN NEW YORK CITY."
"BUT THE BROTHER OF MY MASTER'S FORMER ENEMY TRACKED US DOWN. HE LIVED UP TO HIS NAME, THE SHREDDER, AND KILLED MY MASTER AND HIS BRIDE."
"I ALONE ESCAPED."
"I LEARNED TO FEND FOR MYSELF IN THE ALLEYS AND SEWERS OF THE CITY."
"ONE DAY I CHANCED UPON A SMASHED CANNISTER, WHICH I LATER DISCOVERED HAD CONTAINED RADIOACTIVE WASTE."
T.C.R.I.
"I RESCUED FOUR DIME STORE TURTLES WHO WERE PLAYING BLISSFULLY IN THE GOO AND TOOK THEM TO MY HOME."
T.C.R.

SOMEHOW, THE STRANGE OOZE AFFECTED US. I GREW IN SIZE AND INTELLECT, AS DID THE TURTLES. I RAISED THEM AS MY SONS, NAMING THEM AFTER MY FAVORITE RENAISSANCE ARTISTS:
THEN I TRAINED THEM IN THE ART OF NINJITSU, AND WE AVENGED MY MASTER'S DEATH!
LEONARDO!
MICHAELANGELO!
DONATELLO!
RAPHAEL!
INDEED. AND THE CANNISTER--?
I DO NOT KNOW ITS PRESENT LOCATION. WE HAVE BEEN FORCED TO MOVE OFTEN.
A PITY! PERHAPS YOUR BLOOD STILL HOLDS THE SECRET. MEANWHILE, HOW MAY I MAKE YOUR STAY MORE COMFORTABLE, SPLINTER?
A HOT BATH IS A LUXURY THESE OLD BONES SELDOM GET TO ENJOY.
AHHH! MY SONS WOULD BE JEALOUS TO KNOW THAT I AM SURROUNDED BY SUCH FEMININE BEAUTY!

WE'VE GOT TO GIVE THESE KUNOICHI SOME CREDIT.
THEY'RE PRETTY DAMN GOOD!
YEAH. BUT THEY WEREN'T TRAINED BY THE GREATEST LIVING MASTER OF NINJITSU!
AND WE WERE!
DO YOU THINK YOU CAN MANAGE TO KEEP LEONARDO SAFE BY YOURSELF, MIKEY?
WHY? WHERE DO YOU THINK YOU'RE GOING?
SLICE!

ME? I'VE GOT A DATE TO KEEP!
HOW CAN YOU POSSIBLY THINK OF WOMEN AT A TIME LIKE THIS?
SHEESH! I FEEL LIKE I'M TRAPPED IN A BEER COMMERCIAL THAT COMBINED BAYWATCH AND BARB WIRE!
WHOMP!
WHAK!
C'MON, LEO--WAKE UP!!
THERE ARE TOO MANY OF THESE NINJA BABES! WAKE UP!
HELLO, PIMIKO! I BELIEVE THAT THIS IS OUR DANCE!

I CHOOSE MY OWN PARTNERS!
CRASH
CHING
I THOUGHT MAYBE YOU JUST PREFERRED WOMEN!
TO WHAT? I SEE NO MEN AROUND HERE!
WHAM
ONLY TURTLES! AND BOYS AT THAT!!!
OOPH!
I THINK I'LL THROW YOU BACK, LITTLE TADPOLE--
AND COME BACK FOR YOU IN A FEW YEARS WHEN YOU'RE BIGGER!
NO WAY, BABE! YOU'LL BE TOO OLD FOR ME, THEN!
CHANG
CHANG
CHANG
BESIDES: I'VE GOT A BET WITH MY BROTHER AS TO WHY YOU WEAR A MASK!
INQUIRING MINDS WANT TO KNOW!

IF YOU SO MUCH AS TOUCH ME, YOUR BROTHER WILL DIE!
AW CRAP! THEY GOT TO LEO!
NICE GOING, MIKEY!
NO PROBLEM, groan
YOUR ARROGANCE LED YOU TO CONFRONT ME ALONE!
LEAVING THIS ONE OUTNUMBERED AND VULNERABLE!
YOUR DREAMING BROTHER IS COMING WITH US. ANY QUESTIONS?
JUST ONE!
WHAT IF I DON'T WANT TO GO WITH?
WOMP
"LEO'S BACK!!!"
YOU TURTLES ARE EITHER BLESSED BY THE GODS OR INCREDIBLY LUCKY!

SHE BROKE THE LIGHT BULB! THEY'RE GETTING AWAY AGAIN!
THERE THEY ARE! OOOF! THEY'VE JAMMED THE GATES!
ONE -- TWO--- THREE--- PUSH!
TOO LATE! THEY'RE GONE!
NOT THIS TIME! GET MIKEY AND BE BACK HERE IN TWO MINUTES!
STAY THERE, LEO. I'M COMING AS FAST AS I CAN.
YOU LOOK LIKE A WALKING ARCHERY RANGE!
WAS IT WORTH THIS? DID YOU LOCATE SPLINTER AND DON?
YES!
OKAY THEN. JUST YANK OUT THOSE ARROWS! CAREFULLY!
JUST LIKE ACUPUNCTURE IN REVERSE!

DO YOU SEE WHAT I SEE?
YOU GUYS NEED A LIFT?
WHERE IN BLAZES DID YOU FIND A TRICERATON AIRCAR, RAPH?
I DIDN'T, DONNY DID!
WE FIGURED THAT OUR OLD PAL ZOG STARTED BUILDING IT DURING HIS STAY ON EARTH!
DON FINISHED IT!
TURBINES TO POWER, ENGINES TO SPEED. GET READY TO GO CRUISIN' FOR NINJA CHICKS!
NO!!!
WHY NOT, BOSSMAN?
DON'S IN BAD SHAPE. HIS SHELL IS BUSTED INTO A MILLION PIECES!
HEAD EAST AND FLOOR THIS SUCKER!

DID NOT REALIZE THERE WERE SO MANY ANTHROPOMORPHS IN THE WORLD.
AND MANY MORE WHO HAVE ELUDED ME! BUT NOT FOR LONG. SOMEONE SOMEWHERE HOLDS THE KEY TO SPLICING HUMAN AND ANIMAL DNA!
AND THAT KEY WILL UNLEASH THE POWER OF THE ANCIENT DRAGONS WHICH SLUMBERS INSIDE OF ME!
OME OF THESE LIFE ORMS ARE ALIEN TO IIS REALITY. MANY ORE ARE MUTANTS, OME ARE FRAUDS.
HAW! THIS FORTUNATE OUL TURNED UT TO BE ERELY A MAN IN A YBERNETIC SUIT!
WAS IT NECESSARY TO KILL THEM?
BRUTES! SAVAGE AND BESTIAL IN NATURE, ALMOST ALL OF THEM!
KILLING THESE TORTURED SOULS WAS LIKE AN ACT OF MERCY, LIKE PUTTING A RABID ANIMAL OUT OF ITS MISERY.
I SEE.

IMAGINE MY SURPRISE AT DISCOVERING A HEART AS GENTLE AND CULTURED AS YOURS, SPLINTER.
SO MANY OF YOUR BRETHREN MORE CLOSELY RESEMBLE YOUR FORMER CELL-MATE, MAKO, THE SHARK MAN.
YES, THAT ONE IS EVIL. STILL, PERHAPS YOUR METHODS ARE PARTIALLY TO BLAME?
VIOLENCE BEGETTING VIOLENCE? PERHAPS, BUT--IS SOMETHING AMISS?
THE AIR HERE SMELLS OF BLOOD-- AND DEATH!
THE SMELL OF CARRION, MOSTLY ROAD KILL, FOR MAKO WHO DEMANDED MEAT!
DISGUSTING!
YEAH IT WAS! THE MEAT WAS RANCID AND CRAWLING WITH MAGGOTS.
AND THE PORTIONS WERE TOO SMALL!
EVEN THE GUARD YOU SENT WAS NOTHIN' BUT SKIN AND BONES!
MAKO!!!
WHAM
OOOF!

TOO BAD FOR YOU THAT HE'S UNCONSCIOUS, SHAGGY!
I LIKE TO PLAY WITH MY FOOD!
THERE! IN THAT ALLEY DOWN THERE!
THIS IS THE PLACE. I'M SURE OF IT!
HANG ON, DONATELLO, WE'RE HERE!

YOU SURE THIS IS THE PLACE, LEO? THERE'S NOTHING HERE BUT GARBAGE!
ARE YOU SURE THAT YOU DIDN'T JUST HAVE A BAD DREAM, LEO?
THIS IS THE PLACE. THIS POOL OF BLOODY METAL IS WHERE THE CYBORG SPLATTERED!
OH, JEEZ!
I FOUND HIM!
OR WHAT'S LEFT OF HIM!
I THINK I'M GONNA BARF!
CRAP!
DON! WHAT HAPPENED?!!

FACE FACTS, LEO--
DONATELLO IS DEAD!
YEAH-- THE SCAVENGERS HAVE ALREADY PICKED HIS BONES CLEAN!
BUT I WAS HERE NOT AN HOUR AGO, AND HE WAS ALIVE!

I MEAN, YEAH, HIS SHELL WAS CRUSHED AND HE WAS PARALYZED FROM THE NECK DOWN--
BUT AT LEAST HE WAS STILL ALIVE! AND NOW--
WAIT A MINUTE!
THIS SKELETON--IT HAS FIVE FINGERS AND FIVE TOES!
YOU'RE RIGHT, SHERLOCK, THESE ARE HUMAN BONES. THIS CREEP WAS OVER SIX FEET TALL.
SO, WHO IS THIS?
THERE ARE METAL FRAGMENTS EMBEDDED IN THE BONES. THIS MUST'VE BEEN THE CYBORG DONNY WAS FIGHTING!
BUT WHAT'S HE DOING IN DONNY'S SHELL?

MORE IMPORTANTLY, WHAT IS DON DOING OUT OF HIS SHELL? HE COULDN'T JUST GET UP AND WALK OUT OF IT!
IT'S PART OF HIS BACKBONE AND SPINAL COLUMN!
DON IS HISTORY. IF HE'S NOT COOKING IN A POT OF ROAD-KILL STEW, HE'S HEADED FOR A LAB TABLE IN HANGER 13.
WHEN THIS IS OVER, WE'LL BE BACK TO FIND THE REST OF HIM. IN THE MEANTIME, WE'RE GOING AFTER THOSE RESPONSIBLE FOR THIS!
KRAKLE!
NAMELY THE DRAGONLORD AND THAT NINJA BITCH PIMIKO!
THEY SHOT DONNY, KIDNAPPED HIM AND DUMPED HIM OUT OF A HELICOPTER! THEY'RE GOING TO PAY!
I SWEAR IT!
ME TOO!
AND ME!
LET'S GO!

I STILL CAN'T BELIEVE THAT YOU AND DONATELLO BUILT THIS AIRCAR, RAPH.
WE DIDN'T. ZOG THE TRICERATION STARTED IT. DON MODIFIED AND FINISHED IT.
I MERELY BOOSTED THE PARTS FOR DONNY!
GREAT! AND HOW DID YOU LOCATE THE DRAGONLORD'S HIDEOUT?
RAPH'S PALS IN THE FOOT CLAN CONFIRMED THAT A NINJA BABE NAMED PIMIKO WORKS FOR AN OUTFIT THEY'VE DONE BUSINESS WITH CALLED KOMODO INDUSTRIES!
GET THE CONNECTION: KOMODO DRAGON-- DRAGON LORD?
I CHECKED THE COMPUTER AND KOMODO INC. OWNS A LOT OF LAND HERE IN UPSTATE NEW YORK.
WE'RE HERE! AND WAIT'LL YOU GET A LOAD OF THIS JOINT!

EXCELLENT! PULL OVER AND WE'LL PLAN OUR STRATEGY FOR AN ATTACK LATER TONIGHT!
TONIGHT? WHAT'S WRONG WITH DIVEBOMBING THOSE SUCKERS RIGHT NOW? THEY WON'T KNOW WHAT HIT 'EM!
ARE YOU A NINJA OR JOHN WAYNE? SPLINTER IS IN THERE SOMEWHERE!
YEAH, AND IT'S UP TO US TO RESCUE HIM! ARE YOU CHICKEN, LEO?
SHUT UP!
WHAK!
WE'RE NOT ATTACKING ANYBODY UNTIL WE BURY DONATELLO!
PULL OVER!
OKAY, OKAY. BUT WHAT ABOUT SPLINTER?

"IF HE'S LASTED THIS LONG, ANOTHER FEW HOURS WON'T KILL HIM!"
TOO BAD, RAT. THEY'VE BEEN STARVING ME FOR DAYS: I'M GONNA HAVE TO EAT AND RUN!
I HAVE NO QUARREL WITH YOU, MAKO. LEAVE NOW: FREEDOM IS YOURS!
SAY YOUR PRAYERS, FUZZY--
BECAUSE I'VE ALREADY SAID GRACE!
I CANNOT ALLOW YOU TO HARM EITHER WARLORD KOMODO OR MYSELF, MUCH LESS EAT US!
HAW! AND HOW DO YOU PLAN TO STOP ME ?
LIKE SO.
HAW! A KUNG-FU RAT!

KRAKK!
MY NOSE! YOU BROKE IT, YOU LITTLE RAT-BASTARD!
A TRICK I LEARNED FROM WATCHING JACQUES COUSTEAU!
HE SAID A SHARK'S SNOUT IS MOST SENSITIVE!
I'LL KILL YOU FOR THAT!
I THINK NOT!
GET BACK HERE!
AND NOW I BELIEVE THAT THE CAVALRY HAS ARRIVED!
WHAT THE--? LIZARDS!
BIG LIZARDS, SURROUNDING ME!

THEY'RE ATTACKING FROM ALL DIRECTIONS!
COME AND GET ME, YOU WALKING SUITCASES! I'LL MAKE COWBOY BOOTS OUT OF EACH OF YA!
DO YOU CONTROL YOUR PETS WITH TELEPATHY?
NOT PETS! I TOLD YOU THEY AND I ARE BROTHERS!
I DO NOT CONTROL THEM: I ASK! THEY FIGHT FOR ME WILLINGLY-- AS I MUST NOW AID THEM!
YES. MAKO IS DESTROYING THEM.
THE SHARKMAN MUST DIE! IT WAS A MISTAKE TO--
GASP! PAIN! TERRIBLE PAIN!
NOT NOW, OF ALL TIMES!
DRAGONLORD, ARE YOU ILL?
MY BUSHIDO SPIRIT IS DISEASED! IT BETRAYS ME AGAIN!

I'VE NEVER EATEN MONITOR LIZARD BEFORE!
TASTES KIND OF LIKE CHICKEN!
BUT THEN AGAIN, EVERYTHING TASTES LIKE CHICKEN TO ME!
HA! HA! HA!
SPLINTER-- FLEE WHILE YOU CAN!
QUICKLY. FIND MY BODYGUARDS, THE KUNOICHI!
I WILL NOT LEAVE! I CAN PROTECT YOU MYSELF!
AND WHO'S GONNA PROTECT YOU, RAT?
WOMP!
OW! OW! OW!
MY POOR, BUSTED NOSE!
WHAT'S WRONG WITH CHARLIE CHAN? HE'S HAVING CONVULSIONS!
I DO NOT KNOW.

HE AIN'T SICK! HE'S TRANSFORMING INTO ONE OF THOSE LIZARDS!
THAT WOULDA HAPPENED IN MY STOMACH IF I'D EATEN HIM!
TALK ABOUT A BELLY BUSTER! I'M GONNA BARF!
THIS IS FREAK CITY, RAT! I'M OUTTA HERE!
YOU COMING OR WHAT?
NO. KOMODO TREATED ME AS A GUEST. I WILL SEE TO HIS WELL-BEING.
AND SATISFY MY OWN CURIOSITY.

WARLORD KOMODO, CAN YOU UNDERSTAND ME?
NO, HE CANNOT! IN THIS CONDITION, HE IS LITTLE MORE THAN A MINDLESS BEAST!
AH, YOUR BODYGUARDS HAVE FINALLY ARRIVED, MY FRIEND.
THIS BUTCHERY: IS IT YOUR HANDIWORK, OLD RAT?
WE MUST ACT QUICKLY!
THIS IS MAKO'S HANDIWORK, NOT MINE.
YOU THREE TRACK DOWN THE SHARKMAN. HE CAN'T HAVE GOTTEN VERY FAR!
THE DRAGONLORD SHOULD RECOVER QUICKLY, NOW.
DOES THIS TRANSFORMATION OCCUR OFTEN?
NO MORE QUESTIONS, OLD ONE! NOW THAT YOU KNOW THE TRUTH ABOUT LORD KOMODO'S AFFLICTION--
YOU MUST DIE!

GOOD-BYE, DONNY. WE'RE GONNA MISS YOU, LITTLE BROTHER.
AMEN.

IT'S GETTING LATE. LET'S GO KICK SOME BUTT.
YEAH.
TIME FOR REVENGE.
KRAK
YOU COMING, MIKEY ?
IN A MINUTE, LEO.

HOLD ON, SHORTY!
YONDER LIES THE CASTLE OF OUR ENEMY!
PREPARE FOR THE ASSAULT ON CASTLE KOMODO!
WHAT THE--? MICE!
HUNDREDS OF MICE!
YOW!!
GANGWAY, FREAKS!
LAND SHARK COMIN' THROUGH!

NOW WHY WOULD MICE STAMPEDE?
RUMMBLEE!
VERY SMART MICE!
WHAT THE--?

YIKES! IT'S GODZILLA'S FAMILY!
THEY'RE GIANT MONITOR LIZARDS --ALSO KNOWN AS KOMODO DRAGONS!
BUT THEY'RE NOT INTERESTED IN US!
THEY ONLY HAVE EYES FOR THAT SHARK GUY!
MAYBE THIS IS MY LUCKY DAY, AFTER ALL!
THE KEYS ARE IN THIS HEAP!
HEY! THE AIRCAR!
NO HITCH-HIKERS, YA MUTTS!
THESE THINGS DON'T GIVE UP!
THEY'RE STILL GOING AFTER HIM! THEY MUST HAVE A REAL URGE FOR SEAFOOD!
SO LONG, SUCKERS!

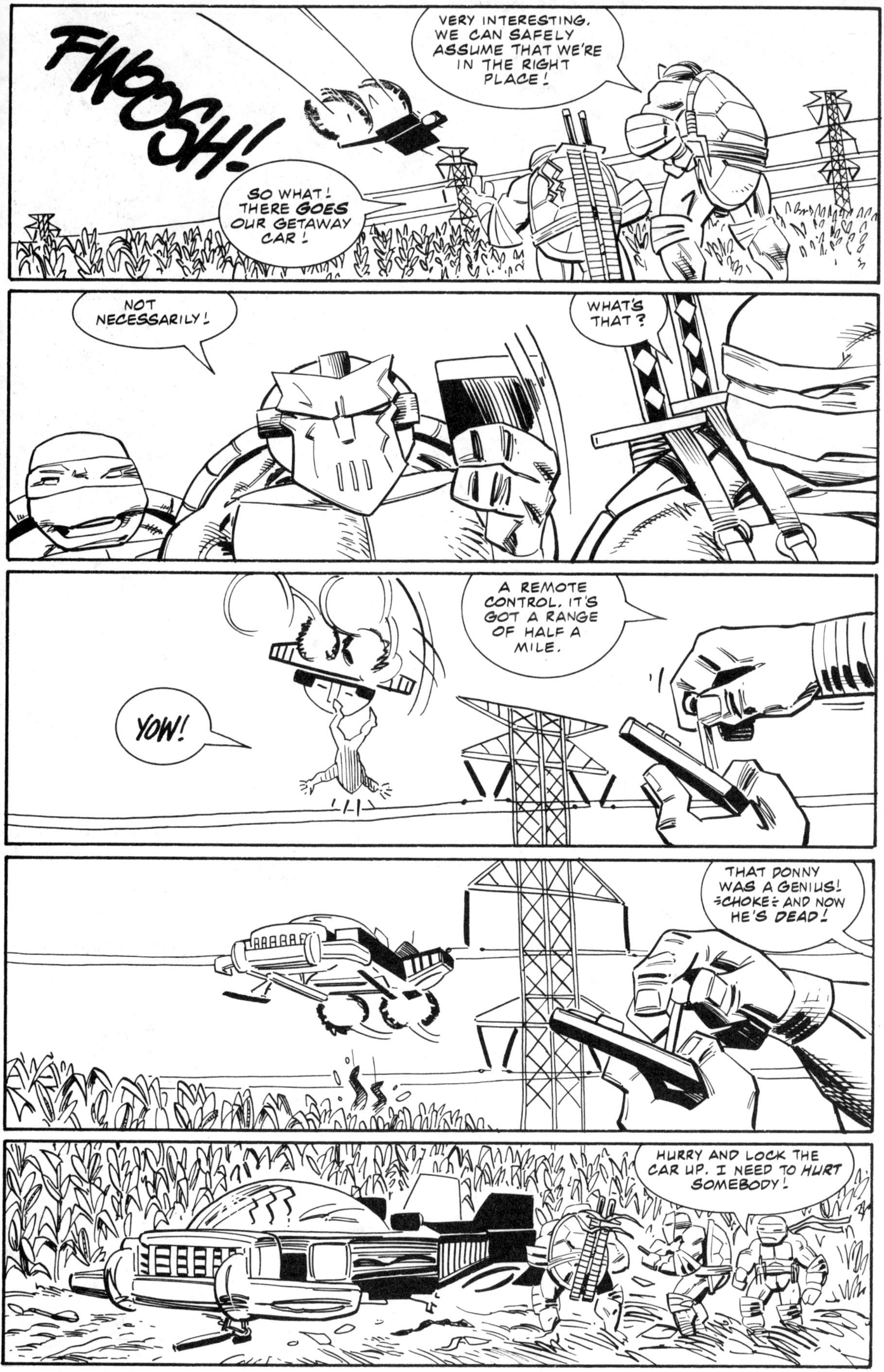
FWOOSH!
VERY INTERESTING. WE CAN SAFELY ASSUME THAT WE'RE IN THE RIGHT PLACE!
SO WHAT! THERE GOES OUR GETAWAY CAR!
NOT NECESSARILY!
WHAT'S THAT?
YOW!
A REMOTE CONTROL. IT'S GOT A RANGE OF HALF A MILE.
THAT DONNY WAS A GENIUS! =CHOKE= AND NOW HE'S DEAD!
HURRY AND LOCK THE CAR UP. I NEED TO HURT SOMEBODY!

SPEAKING OF DONATELLO--
IS SOMEBODY THERE?
HELLO?
THERE'S THAT NOISE AGAIN!
I WISH I COULD MOVE! I CAN'T SEE ANYTHING BUT THAT STREET LAMP!
=GASP= SOMEBODY IS THERE!
BUT WHO--?
MUTANT TARGET STILL LIVES!
TARGET?
TERMINATION IS IMMINENT!
GROSS! IT'S THE CYBORG THAT FELL OUT OF THE COPTER WITH ME!
PAIN! SO MUCH PAIN, TEARING ME APART! IT'S KILLING ME!
I'M-- BLACKING OUT-- AGAIN.
=GASP= I'M ALIVE?!
WAS THAT A DREAM? NO-- I REMEMBER, IT REALLY HAPPENED!

I'M MOVING! THE CYBORG MUST BE TAKING ME SOMEWHERE! I STILL CAN'T MOVE, BUT IT LOOKS LIKE WE'RE GOING THROUGH A --
CORNFIELD?
SILENCE!
SENSORS INDICATE MULTIPLE CARBON-BASED LIFEFORMS AHEAD.
SWITCHING TO INFRARED: SUBJECTS HAVE BEEN LOCATED.
FIVE DECEASED, ONE LIVING.
LIVING SUBJECT IS DEVOURING THE DECEASED.
CHOMP CHOMP URP
RUN FOR YOUR LIFE, BUDDY!
SILENCE, MUTANT.
WHO THE -- ? WHAT'RE YOU LOOKIN' AT, BUTTHEAD?
IN FACT, WHAT ARE YOU?
SUBJECT IS DANGEROUS. LOCKING TARGET.
FIRE.
ZAP!
THE CYBORG BLASTED THAT POOR GUY!

I CAN MOVE NOW! GASP! BUT THAT GUN-- IT'S ATTACHED TO MY ARM!
I'M THE CYBORG!
BUT HOW--?
HOW?!

THAT'S THE LAST OF THE GUARDS! LET'S DRAG THEM INTO THE WOODS AND TIE THEM UP!
DC
YOU WON'T NEED TO WASTE ANY ROPE ON THIS ONE!
HERE WE GO AGAIN!
ARE YOU DEAF, RAPH? I SAID NO KILLING!
WISE UP, LEO: THIS IS WAR!
THEY'LL GET LOOSE AND WE'LL HAVE TO ICE THEM LATER ANYWAY!
WAR? WE DON'T KNOW WHAT WE'LL FIND IN THE CASTLE!
WHAT?!
CLIMBING CLAWS ON. LET'S GO.

I CAN SEE ALL OF THE COMPOUND FROM HERE. IT'S A REGULAR FORTRESS!
THERE ARE MORE GUARDS AROUND THE INSIDE PERIMETER--
-- AND THE KUNOICHI NINJA BABES PATROL THE INTERIOR! NO SIGN OF PIMIKO, THOUGH.
THESE CLOWNS KILLED DONATELLO AND KIDNAPPED SPLINTER!
WHAT DO YOU THINK WE'LL FIND IN THERE--
WAIT! THERE SHE IS INSIDE THE CASTLE WITH--
OH CRAP!
SPLINTER SIPPING TEA WITH WARLORD KOMODO ?!
WHAT IS IT ?
?
SEE FOR YOURSELF.
WELL ? IS IT BAD?
YES!
SEE FOR YOURSELF, MIKEY.
SHHH!
WE'VE FOUND MASTER SPLINTER!
HE'S HAVING TEA WITH WARLORD KOMODO!

PLEASE, MY FRIEND, EAT. YOU HAVE MY WORD OF HONOR THAT THAT THE FOOD IS NOT POISONED.
AH. AND YET I AM STILL TO DIE BECAUSE I KNOW TOO MUCH?
UNFORTUNATELY, YES.
IN ALL CORNERS OF THE WORLD, MY ARMIES TRAIN IN THE NAME OF THE DRAGONLORD!
PREPARING FOR THE WAR THAT WILL RESTORE THE DRAGON BUSHIDO TO JAPAN'S IMPERIAL THRONE FOR THE FIRST TIME IN 400 YEARS!
MY ANCESTRAL BIRTHRIGHT!
AND YOU ALONE KNOW MY TRAGIC SECRET-- THAT MY SACRED BUSHIDO SPIRIT IS ACCURSED!
THAT INSTEAD OF WIELDING THE POWER OF A MYTHICAL WYRM, YOU BECOME A GIANT LIZARD--
--A MINDLESS BEAST LIKE YOUR BROTHERS HERE?
YOU OF ALL SOULS SHOULD REALIZE THAT ANIMALS ARE NOT STUPID! WERE YOU YOURSELF NOT THE PET OF HAMATO YOSHI, SPLINTER-- PRIOR TO YOUR OWN AMAZING TRANSFORMATION?
STILL, YOU ARE CORRECT. MY FOLLOWERS WILLINGLY FOLLOW THE LEGEND, AND I PREFER NOT TO DISAPPOINT THEM WITH THE TRUTH.

SO I MUST BECOME THE LEGEND! LUCKILY MY SCIENTISTS HAVE SYNTHESIZED THE MUTAGEN FROM TRACES IN YOUR BLOOD.
I AM-- DIZZY. THE FOOD-- IT WAS POISONED?
NO, MERELY DRUGGED.
I DID NOT BELIEVE YOU WOULD GO WILLINGLY TO YOUR GRAVE TO KEEP MY SECRET.
YOU ARE-- WITHOUT-- HONOR.
I FIND HONOR TO BE AN OVER-RATED VIRTUE. I TRUST ONLY IN POWER.
TAKE HIM TO THE LABORATORY!
I KNEW IT! LET'S GO!
IT'S CLOBBERIN' TIME!
SOMETHING IS SCREWY!
SPLINTER JUST PASSED OUT AND SOME GOONS ARE DRAGGING HIM AWAY!

ELSEWHERE...
I CAN'T BELIEVE IT!!
SOMEHOW I'VE BEEN TRANSFORMED INTO SOME KIND OF WEIRD-ASS CYBORG!
NO!
YOU'RE MY PRISONER, REPTILE!
THAT VOICE! IT'S SO FAMILIAR! WHERE'VE I HEARD IT BEFORE?
GET MOVING, FREAK! THE DRAGONLORD IS WAITING FOR YOU!
WHAT THE--?
I KNOW! YOU'RE THE CYBORG WITH THE LIVING ARMOR THAT SHOT AND KIDNAPPED ME!
THE OTHER PRISONER IS ESCAPING! SHOOT IT!
SHOOT IT! SHOOT IT!
NO! LET HIM GO!
I'M IN CHARGE NOW, AND I WANT TO KNOW JUST WHAT THE HELL IS GOING ON!!

GET UP! HUNT DOWN THE SHARKMAN!
WHY WON'T THE ARMOR FOLLOW MY ORDERS? GET UP, DAMMIT!
SHUT UP, WILL YA?! I'M TRYING TO FIGURE THIS OUT!
"I REMEMBER GETTING SHOT BY YOU AND YOUR CYBORG BUDDIES!
"I WOKE UP AND ATTACKED YOU--
"UNFORTUNATELY, WE WERE IN A HELICOPTER AND FELL OUT!
"WE FOUGHT AND I BLEW YOUR HEAD OFF WITH YOUR OWN GUN!
"I HIT THE GROUND-- HARD! I BROKE MY SHELL --AND MY BACK. I COULDN'T MOVE!
"THEN YOU-- WHAT WAS LEFT OF YOU-- CRAWLED OVER AND SAID--
HOST BODY IS TERMINATED! MUST LOCATE NEW HOST--
--OR EXTINCTION IS IMMINENT!
"THEN THE METAL ARMOR-- IT CRAWLED FROM YOUR BODY TO MINE--
"--LIKE A GIANT SWARM OF ANTS!
"THE LIVING METAL ENTERED MY WOUNDS --FUSED WITH ME-- HURT ME--
"IT HEALED ME: BECAME A PART OF ME! I PASSED OUT!"
NO! IT'S A LIE! IT'S IMPOSSIBLE! I'M NOT DEAD! IT'S MY ARMOR!
NOT ANYMORE, PAL!

YOU DON'T GET IT, DO YOU? YOU'RE DEAD, PAL! DECEASED, DEFUNCT, KAPUT! YOU'RE WORM FOOD!
ALL THAT'S LEFT OF YOU IS A BAD MEMORY-- AND I'M GOING TO ERASE IT!
NO!!
COMPUTER, DELETE ALL DATA CONCERNING THE PREVIOUS HOST ORGANISM!
NOOOOOOOO
HASTA LA VISTA, CREEP! AND YOU GET LOST TOO, COMPUTER! IF I WANT YOUR HELP I'LL ASK FOR IT.
MUCH BETTER! NOW I CAN HEAR MYSELF THINK!
THE ARMOR'S MEMORY TELLS ME THAT THIS IS THE DRAGONLORD'S CASTLE DEAD AHEAD!
FIRST I'LL FIGURE OUT HOW THIS ARMOR WORKS! THEN I'LL PAY A VISIT TO WARLORD KOMODO, AND FIND OUT JUST WHAT'S GOING ON.
AND HE'D BETTER HAVE SOME DAMN GOOD ANSWERS!

THE MUTAGEN EXTRACT IS READY!
I AM TOLD THAT THE SERUM MAY KILL YOU, OR POSSIBLY MUTATE YOU BEYOND RECOGNITION!
I SALUTE YOU, SPLINTER, AND REGRET THAT EVENTS CONSPIRED AGAINST OUR FRIENDSHIP.
STOP!
I MUST SPEAK WITH THE RAT FIRST!
YOU ARE WASTING PRECIOUS TIME, PIMIKO!
FORGIVE ME, WARLORD, BUT EARLIER YOU MENTIONED HAMATO YOSHI. WHAT IS YOUR CONNECTION WITH YOSHI, OLD RAT ?
HE WAS MY --MASTER. I CARRY ON HIS WORK.
I HAVE BEEN TOLD THAT YOSHI'S CLAN IS RESPONSIBLE FOR THE DEATH OF MY FATHER! IS THIS TRUE?
HIS NAME WAS OROKU SAKI?
SHREDDER?! YOU ARE HIS DAUGHTER?!
YES. MY MOTHER FLED FROM HIM BEFORE I WAS BORN! THE WARLORD GAVE US REFUGE!

THEN YOU KNOW THAT YOUR FATHER WAS EVIL INCARNATE! HE DESERVED TO DIE!
I KNOW ONLY THAT HE WAS MURDERED!
STAND ASIDE, PIMIKO. YOUR FATHER'S ENEMY WILL SOON CEASE TO EXIST! THAT IS AN ORDER!
NO! I DEMAND THE RIGHT TO FACE HIM IN COMBAT!
THERE IS NO TIME! MY WISHES TAKE PRECEDENCE AND THE SERUM MUST BE TESTED!
BESIDES, I HAVE NO DESIRE TO LOSE YOUR SERVICES. YOU ARE GOOD--BUT THE RAT IS BETTER!
INJECT HIM WITH THE MUTAGEN, DR. WU!
NOT SO FAST, WU!
YEAH-- WE WANT A SECOND OPINION!
SKRASH!
THE TURTLES!!

DID YOU MISS ME, PIMIKO?
FOOL! YOUR INTERFERENCE HAS DOOMED YOUR MASTER!
KILL THE INTERLOPERS, MY KUNOICHI-- AND PIMIKO ALSO, IF SHE INTERFERES!
MY NAME IS ALL THAT I OWN, WARLORD! I CHOOSE HONOR ABOVE POWER!
GASP!
MY VENGEANCE WILL NOT BE DENIED, NOT EVEN BY YOU!
DID I MISS SOMETHING, PIMIKO? WHY ARE YOU HELPING US?
SHUT UP AND FREE YOUR SENSEI!
"ALL THAT MATTERS IS THAT HE DOES NOT DIE HERE TODAY!"
RAWR

QUICKLY! YOU CAN ESCAPE THIS WAY! THE TUNNEL LEAD TO A CAVERN IN THE HILLS!
MASTER-- CAN YOU WALK?
I AM-- DIZZY, MY SON--BUT I CAN MANAGE!
HURRY!
WAIT FOR US IN THE CAVES, MASTER. I MUST HELP MY BROTHERS.
I SHALL TRY--
PIMIKO--CAN'T YOU JUST CALL OFF YOUR NINJA BABES? WE DON'T NEED TO FIGHT AT ALL!
THE KUNOICHI ARE LOYAL ONLY TO THE DRAGONLORD! THEY WILL NO LONGER HEED ME!
I AM A TRAITOR!
I WILL NOT ATTACK THEM, BUT NEITHER WILL I ALLOW THEM TO PURSUE YOUR MASTER!
SUIT YOURSELF!
IT'S ABOUT TIME YOU DECIDED TO LEND A HAND!
HEY-- SPLINTER IS SAFE AND PIMIKO IS OUT OF THE FIGHT!
DO I HAVE TO DO EVERYTHING AROUND HERE?

THE MONITOR LIZARD-- IT MUTATED!!
THAT MEANS THEY'RE PLAYING WITH MUTAGEN!
DO NOT KILL THEM, MY BROTHER-- WE HAVE LOST THE RAT! THEIR BLOOD IS OUR SALVATION!
MUTAGEN?! WHAT WILL IT DO TO SPLINTER?!
GOT TO WORRY ABOUT HIM LATER! FIRST LET'S WRECK THIS T-REX!
HE'S A MONITOR LIZARD, NOT A DINOSAUR!
EITHER WAY, HE'S GONNA BE EXTINCT!
WHAM
OOOF!

HE GOT RAPH! AND HIS SKIN IS LIKE STEEL! MY 'CHUCKS JUST BOUNCE OFF!
WHOOPS!
MY BLADES ARE DRAWING BLOOD!
AIM FOR HIS BELLY OR NECK! THEY'RE BOUND TO BE THE MOST VULNERABLE SPOTS!
YOU CANNOT HURT ME--
--WITHOUT YOUR PUNY WEAPONSSS!
CRIPES! IT CAN TALK!
GOOD! MAYBE WE CAN DISCUSS THINGS OVER COFFEE!
NO MORE TALK! NOW YOU DIE!
BUT KOMODO WANTS US ALIVE!
TOO BAD!

AAARGH!
SPLAT! SPLAT! SPLAT!
I SEE IT-- BUT I DON'T BELIEVE IT!
IT'S DONATELLO! HE'S ALIVE!!
EAT HOT LEAD, KOMODO!
CHOOM CHOOM CHOOM
HOW DO YOU LIKE BEING INVADED BY TRIGGER-HAPPY CYBORGS?

REMEMBER ME, GIRLS? YOU KIDNAPPED ME, ALONG WITH MY MASTER! HIS NAME IS SPLINTER --HE'S A RAT!
WHERE IS HE?
FANCY MEETING YOU GUYS HERE!
DON'T GET UPSET, BUT WE ALREADY RESCUED SPLINTER!
DONNY-- THANK GOD! WE THOUGHT YOU WERE DEAD!
SO DID I, GUYS. SO DID I.
RUMMBLE
NOW WHAT?!
THE WHOLE JOINT IS FALLING APART!
WARLORD KOMODO INITIATED THE SELF-DESTRUCT MECHANISM!
WE'VE GOT THREE MINUTES TO GET OUT OF HERE!
LET'S GO!

AREN'T YOU COMING, PIMIKO?
NO. SOME OF MY KUNOICHI ARE MERELY WOUNDED! I MUST TRY TO SAVE THEM TOO!
HEY!!
SLAM
IT'S A TRAP!
NO SWEAT-- I'VE GOT A LIGHT! SHOULD WE GO BACK!
NO--WE'VE ALREADY ACCOMPLISHED WHAT WE SET OUT TO DO! LET'S CATCH UP THE MASTER SPLINTER!
WHAT'S THAT MOVING UP AHEAD OF US? SOME KIND OF FOG--?
FOG NOTHING! THAT'S A SWARM OF BATS --HUNDREDS OF THEM!
AND THEY'RE COMING THIS WAY!

OUCH! EVERYBODY HIT THE DECK! AND DOUSE YOUR LIGHT, DONNY --
IT'S SPOOKING THEM!
THEN WE'RE EVEN! BATS GIVE ME THE CREEPS!
THAT'S BETTER! EVERYBODY HOLD HANDS -- LET'S CRAWL FOR A WAYS!
I SEE SOMETHING AHEAD! DONNY--?
FLAME ON!
SKREE! SKREE! LIGHT BURNS!
SICK!
GASP! A GIANT BAT-THING!
SKREE! NOT HURT SPLIN-TERRR!

TIME FOR A LITTLE TARGET PRACTICE!
NO!! DON'T SHOOT!
YOU SHOULD'VE LET ME PLUG THAT THING, LEO! WHAT A MONSTER!
AT LEAST WE KNOW THAT IT DIDN'T HURT SPLINTER! I WONDER WHERE HE IS?
ARE YOU GUYS BLIND?
THAT BAT-THING WAS SPLINTER!
LEO'S RIGHT! KOMODO PUMPED SPLINTER FULL OF MUTAGEN AND SOMEHOW HE'S BEEN TRANSFORMED INTO A BAT!
IT SOUNDS CRAZY, BUT IT'S THE ONLY EXPLANATION!
OH NO! HE FLEW AWAY! C'MON-- WE'VE GOT TO FIND HIM!
WE'LL CATCH HIM IN THE AIRCAR! LUCKY WE KEPT IT PARKED NEARBY!
HE WENT SOUTH!
YES'M, MISS DAISY.
HOW LONG HAS IT BEEN SINCE WE HIGH-TAILED IT OUT OF THE CASTLE? MAYBE PIMIKO WAS B.S.'ING US ABOUT THE SELF DESTRUCT DEVICE?

BRAKKABADOOM!
NEVER MIND.
CRAP! THE EXPLOSION DROVE THE OTHER BATS OUT OF THE CAVES! WE CAN'T FOLLOW THEM ALL! WE'VE LOST SPLINTER!
THEN LET'S HEAD FOR HOME! MAYBE SPLINTER WILL COME TO TO HIS SENSES AND GO THERE TOO!
I'VE GOT JUST ONE QUESTION?
WHAT'S THAT, DON?
ISN'T ANYBODY GONNA ASK WHAT THE HECK HAPPENED TO ME?
THE END--FOR NOW!

MATSUDA
MENDOZA
BULLS NBA CHAMPS